Mr Big

Ed Vere

Let me tell you a story about a friend of mine, he goes by the name of Big... Mr Big.

Now, Mr Big had a small problem. Compared to everyone else, he was extremely...

PUFFIN

...big!

He was **so big** that
anywhere he went,
all everyone saw was
someone **big** and **scary.**

No one stuck around to find out
who he **really** was. So inside,
Mr Big felt very,

very small.

And that's how it **always** was.

When **Mr Big**
went to the cafe…

...everyone had
other things to do.

When Mr Big
got on the bus,
everybody else
got off.

And when he went to the pool,
well, let's just say,
everyone needed to be...

...**somewhere** else.

No one ever saw the **real Mr Big**.

One day, Mr Big
noticed a piano
in a shop window.

It looked all alone.

Just like him.

So he bought it
and took it home.

As **Mr Big** sat alone at the piano,
he thought of **all** the things
that made him sad.

And then he played.

His music drifted out through the open window
and into the evening sky. It drifted across
the rooftops, over to his neighbours.

And they wondered who was playing
such beautiful music?

The word spread,
and night after night
everyone came from all over town.
And still no one knew who was playing.
It was a big mystery.

But inside,
Mr Big was still alone.

And then, one morning,
Mr Big received his first ever letter.

It was an invitation,
and it said...

Dear Mystery

Thank you for
music. Everyone':
for weeks, and
~~the~~ **one** thing..
We'd love to meet

Me and a couple
playing tonight a
Please come and

See you later?

A friend.

Pianist,

your ~~funky~~ beautiful
~~b~~een listening to you.
~~w~~e're all wondering
who are you?
you!

~~o~~f the guys are ~~jam~~
~~t~~he ~~four~~ Blue Note.
~~j~~oin our band!

That night Mr Big joined the band.
All night long the joint was jumping
and nobody wanted to leave!

At last, everyone could see
the real Mr Big.

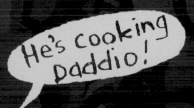

Now that the **Big Band** has hit **the big** time
and **everyone** wants to meet them,
Mr Big has a **new** problem.
He doesn't get much time to be alone...

and that's **just** the way he likes it!

A very BIG thank you
to Mandy Suhr!

PUFFIN BOOKS
Published by the Penguin Group:
London, New York, Australia, Canada, India,
Ireland, New Zealand and South Africa
Penguin Books Ltd, Registered Offices:
80 Strand, London WC2R 0RL, England

puffinbooks.com

First published 2008
004 - 10 9 8 7 6 5 4
Text and illustrations copyright © Ed Vere, 2008
The moral right of the author/illustrator
has been asserted
Printed in China
ISBN: 978–0–141–50060–7

edvere.com